First American Edition published in 2009 by Enchanted Lion Books,
201 Richards Street, Studio 4, Brooklyn, NY 11231

Originally published in Dutch as Boos by Sarah Verroken, © Clavis, 2007

Translated by Sarah Verroken

[A CIP record is on file with the Library of Congress]

ISBN-10: 1-59270-083-7
ISBN-13: 978-1-59270-083-7
Printed in Slovenia

Sarah Verroken

FEELING SAD

SAD

ENCHANTED LION BOOKS
NEW YORK

Duck is taking a walk with her little toy Cuddly. But she is not having a good time. Everything around her seems so gloomy.

Dark clouds hang over her head. Everything looks black—even the flowers. Duck is grumpy... and sad.

Duck feels like hiding in a small corner with Cuddly under her wing. Why is she so sad?

"Hey, what's happening?" Duck looks up. Drops fall from the sky. Could the clouds be sad too? Duck feels worse than ever.

"No pluck, Duck?" ribbits a tiny frog.
"Cheer up. Look ahead!"

Duck wonders, "Could Frog be right?"
She looks around and spots a teeny
tiny bit of color.
"Yes!" Duck quacks. "I can see it's getting
brighter!"

"Cuddly!" shouts Duck.
"We have to move on!
We have to do something now!"

Quack-quacking away, Duck gathers the clouds together. "Clouds," she says firmly, "let's search for the sun!"

"Come back, Sun!" Duck calls.
"It's time to warm the flowers
and dry up all our tears.
We have been feeling sad long enough!"

Duck looks for the sun. Is it hiding in the grass? Duck waddles around, searching everywhere, but it's the sun that finds Duck first, shining warmly down upon her.

Duck is so happy!
The flowers are bright again,
the water sparkles and
Duck can see her own
wonderfully yellow self.

"How beautiful everything is,"
Duck smiles, and the butterfly on
her bill fully agrees.